But the fruit the Holy Spirit
produces is love,
joy and peace. It is being patient,
kind and good.
It is being faithful and gentle
and having control of oneself.
—Galatians 5:22-23

ZONDERKIDZ

Pups of the Spirit
Copyright © 2014 by Jill Gorey and Nancy Haller
Illustrations © 2014 by Deborah Melmon

This title is also available as a Zondervan ebook.
Visit www.zondervan.com/ebooks.

Requests for information should be addressed to:
Zonderkidz, *Grand Rapids, Michigan 49530*

ISBN 978-0-310-73061-3

Scriptures taken from the Holy Bible, *New International Reader's Version*®, NIrV®.
Copyright© 1995, 1996, 1998 by Biblica, Inc.™ Used by permission of Zondervan.
All rights reserved worldwide.

Contributors: *Jill Gorey and Nancy Haller*
Editor: *Barbara Herndon*
Art direction and design: *Cindy Davis*

Printed in China

14 15 16 17 /LPC/ 10 9 8 7 6 5 4 3 2 1

Dedicated to
**Kathy, Jeanne,
and Annie.**

—D. M.

Max

Peanut

Pete

Frankie

Joy

Pups of the Spirit

illustrated by Deborah Melmon

Gigi

Kay

Squeaky

Goose

ZONDERkidz

Wiggly-waggly pups in a pile,

add up to nine if they wag single file.

God gave each puppy a gift of its own,
and **PUPS OF THE SPIRIT** is how they are known!

These pups show us how God wants us to be—
each with a special trait he likes to see.

These heavenly hounds are so cuddly and fun,
let's meet all the puppies right now, one by one!

Max is a pup whose heart's filled with **LOVE.**
He was given this gift from the good Lord above.

He's a great friend to others, a warm, fuzzy pooch,
and his favorite greeting's a big, sloppy smooch!

Joy

Joy is SO happy and full of good cheer …
though you might not know by the way she appears.

Her face may be stuck in a permanent scowl,
but this pup is JOYFUL!

You won't hear *her* growl.

Peace

This is a calm, mellow basset named Pete ...
as **PEACEFUL** a pup as you'll ever meet.

Pete doesn't worry, Pete doesn't fight.
He's so filled with **PEACE** ...

he's out like a light!

Z Z Z Z Z

This hot dog won't stress if something is late.
He knows things take time, and he's happy to wait.

Peanut is PATIENT. He doesn't mind sitting ...
and waiting for Kay to be done with her knitting.

If you're looking for **KINDNESS**, then you must meet Kay …
who loves to knit gifts and then give them away!

And when they don't fit, most are too **KIND** to say!

Goodness

The gift of **GOODNESS** was given to Goose.
And he, like his heart, is as big as a moose!

This pup enjoys helping and doing **GOOD** deeds,
and he'll lend a paw to others in need.

Faithfulness

Last seen chasing a squirrel

LOST PUP.

Frankie

Frankie is **FAITHFULNESS**, through and through;
a dalmatian—dependable, loyal, and true.

If you're in a tough "spot", she won't run and hide.
You can count on this pup to stay right by your side.

Gentleness

This little puffball, so fluffy and fair,
treats all of God's creatures with soft, tender care.

Gigi is loving and so very GENTLE;
her warmhearted ways are not accidental.

Self-Control

Time to meet Squeaky, the last of the bunch.
This pup's favorite thing is a nice bone to crunch.
When Pete dozes off leaving one in his bowl,
he's thankful that Squeaky displays **SELF-CONTROL**.

Nine Pups of the Spirit, nine friends that are new,
nine traits that God loves and gave to us too!
Nine gifts that will keep us from losing our way,
and help us to be more like him every day.